TRILOGY OF EVE BOOK 1.5

HEART OF EVE

PAM GODWIN

This novella was written as an introduction to the
Trilogy of Eve.

This can be read first or as bonus material between the
other books in the trilogy.
It chronologically falls midway through Book 1.

The trilogy is a continuous story of interconnected
standalones.
The following must be read in order:

Dead of Eve #1
Blood of Eve #2
Dawn of Eve #3

"This story takes you on an extraordinary journey of survival, heartbreak, love, and edge of your seat thrills. Between the spectacular writing, the amazing sex—God, the sex was even more than I could ever imagine in my wildest fantasies—and a unique plot layered with so much depth and emotion you won't be able to put this book down."

~*Love Between the Sheets*

ONE

Prayer was one way to cope with the end of the world. The lethal edge of my sword was another. Either might've saved me from the five-and-a-half-feet of temptation that slept in my bed. But I'd brought her here, invited her into my underground bunker to give her a safe place to hide, and now I never wanted her to leave. In a way, I'd already surrendered.

She would argue our paths had crossed by coincidence, but I believed divine intervention had sent her to this desolate town. A town in the arse end of England that hadn't seen the likes of a woman since the plague hit nineteen months ago. Rumor was, only ten percent of humanity remained worldwide. The rest were mutated creatures. No children or elderly survived. No women.

Except Evie.

The night I met her, she confirmed the rumors in her American accent. She would know better than most, having traveled halfway across the world, alone, and searching for answers about her mysterious survival.

I glanced at the mattress, enthralled, as she

stretched her toned limbs, her arms folding beneath the pillow and pulling it against her angelic face. Waves of blonde hair fell around her dainty shoulders and ribs. A single candle cast a warm glow over her closed eyes, her breaths soft and hypnotic. Still asleep.

Beside the bed, I turned back to the prayer bench and bowed my head, my knees digging into the worn padding on the kneeler. This was the second time tonight I'd shlunked away from her body heat, tight backside, and intoxicating feminine scent. Was that what sex smelled like? Hot and drugging? Sweet and tempting?

Bloody hell, she was a persistent test of my obedience. Neither distance nor prayer had softened the steely ache between my legs. In what universe could a man resist the strength and beauty that embodied this woman?

I must've pissed off God. Maybe it was all those pervy thoughts I'd conjured about Sister Agnes in secondary school? Why else would He so sadistically torture me by sending the last surviving woman to my doorstep? A woman who could lure Jesus Himself into tasting the forbidden fruit.

As fierce as she was with guns and knives, maybe she didn't need my protection from the blood-sucking monsters that haunted the crumbled foundations aboveground, but God knew I needed her. I needed human interaction, affection, a link to the benevolent life I'd lost. She was my escape from the isolation of this brutal world. Even if it meant challenging the celibacy I'd desperately held my entire life.

I focused on the crucifix that hung above the bench, mouthing the prayers I knew by rote, my fingers gliding over the rosary beads. I needed to remember she trusted me. Or rather, she trusted my black button-down cassock and white collar. In the month she'd been here, she'd spoken candidly about the dangers she'd faced on her travels, the most vicious being the men who hunted her. She feared humans far more than the snarling, infected mutations.

I promised her I would protect her from men, but who would protect her from me? My control was as fragile as the string connecting the beads in my hand. She only needed to pull, ever-so-slightly, and I would break.

My gaze wandered back to the bed, snagging on her parted lips, the sensual curve of her shoulder, and the neckline of her shirt where it slipped downward, clinging precariously to the taut peak of her nipple.

I looked away and scrubbed a hand over my face as more heat rushed south, gathering and throbbing below the waistband of my briefs. The cotton stretched so bloody tight it threatened to tear the bollix off me.

"Roark?"

Her sleepy whisper floated across my skin, caressing places no woman had ever touched. The sensation filled me with wonderment. Hunger. Guilt.

I clenched my hands and drew a calming breath. "Mm?"

She sat up and leaned against the wall, her fingers straightening the shirt to cover her chest. "Can't sleep?"

"Nah." I stared straight at her. At the glowing hope for mankind's future. At the devastating threat to my vow. "Just praying, love."

She licked her bottom lip, and I felt it like a jolt along my shaft. Jaysus fuck. Could she see my standing prick? I dropped my arm to block her view.

Her gaze followed the movement, her mouth bowing downward in an expression of regret. "Because of me again?" She scooted to the far edge of the bed. "I should go. This isn't right."

Same thing she said every day. Made my heart clench every bloody time.

I climbed onto the bed behind her, hooked an arm around her waist, and settled us on our sides.

She twisted in my embrace, chest to chest, blinking those bewitching golden eyes as she stared up at me. "I can feel your… Dammit, Roark." She angled her hips away from mine and glanced across the open room. "I'm going to start sleeping on the couch."

"The fuck you will." I tightened my arm around her back, stalling her attempts to escape and torturing my damned self-control. "You think I didn't get chubbed up before I met you?"

"I think…" She sighed, relenting in my hold, and touched her forehead to mine. "I think you slept in your bed without worrying about your vow."

"I slept alone. I had *no one*. A fate worse than temptation."

"Maybe."

She grazed her lips across my cheek, and I savored the connection, let it shiver down my spine.

4

She didn't linger, straining against my arm until I released her. Her reluctance had everything to do with my vow. She wanted this, wanted *us*. She'd made that painfully clear in the way she stared at my body and slumped her shoulders whenever I rejected her. She didn't want to be the woman who made me hate myself for foregoing my faith.

Sliding off the mattress, she backed away and tugged the hem of the shirt around her bare thighs. "I'm going to the surface today."

Another thing she said every day.

"No." I threw my legs over the side of the bed, ready to tackle her if she attempted to run.

We'd only left the bunker once since she'd arrived. Solar panels on the homes above provided minimal electricity and hot water underground. Food storage would last another few weeks. All of it was here when I'd stumbled upon the dodgy place. Though not too dodgy compared to the desolation gnawing away the brick and mortar of every town I'd passed since leaving Northern Ireland a year ago.

"I need more clothes." She dug through the hangers and looked at me over her shoulder. "Everything I brought here is too small."

"We can tailor the trousers we have."

When I'd found her, she was as thin as a streak of piss. She'd eaten well under my care, her curves filling out and her creamy skin flushed with health. She was the sexiest woman I'd ever seen, and I couldn't find the strength to withdraw my greedy gaze from the round rise of her arse. I knew it was wrong, looking at her the way I did. Thinking about her small frame writhing beneath the demand of my desire. Imagining how the clasp of her body would suck me in. I'd gone thirty-two years without stroking myself, but after living with her for a month, it was all I could do to keep my hands out of my scunders.

God, please tell me what to do with this woman. Give me a sign, a token of strength, something to show me how to proceed.

Pivoting toward me, she anchored her fists on her hips, and her gaze lowered, narrowed on my groin.

Hard and pulsing and tenting my briefs, I couldn't hide it. "My thoughts are harmless, love. Doesn't violate my vow."

"Well, it should. Ugh. You don't get it." She swung back to the hangers and pulled out a ratty pair of jeans. "The way you look at me, your sexy as hell accent, and dammit, you never wear a shirt..." She stared at the ceiling. "What kind of priest has an eight-pack?" She dropped her head, letting it fall against her hand. "I can't do this. You're a fucking tease."

And she was a temptress. She didn't even have to try. With each shift of her hips, shared glance, and breathy sigh, the leash on my vow slipped that much further from my grasp.

"We've been cooped up too long." She looked around the open room, her gaze tracing the concrete worktop that lined the far wall, the plaid couch sprawled in the center, the bathroom door, the prayer bench, and paused on the bed. "Neither of us have had privacy for weeks. We're on top of each other. If we don't get out of here for a while, we're going to be on top, under, and *in* each other."

Blunt and so very fecking probable, her words found me, gripped me, and made me impossibly harder.

God, now would be a really good time to answer my prayers. Is she here as a test of my devotion to you? You have my heart on the altar. But I am only human, and she's my ultimate weakness. Please God, help me see if I'm taking liberties with her that you don't approve of.

"I need answers." She tucked her hair behind her ear. "There might be people out there who know things. Survivors like us. Please, Roark."

It was doubtful. People were dying, and the few who lived would more likely hurt her than give her answers. On the slim chance she found a good man who could explain why she survived when no other women did, then what? Would he offer her the one thing I couldn't?

She wasn't just a stunning woman. She was a potently sexual one. I saw it in her eyes when she thought I wasn't looking. Felt it in the clench of her thighs when we lay beneath the blankets. Heard it in her muffled moans when she touched herself behind the bathroom door. She wanted sex, and she was stuck with a priest.

But she didn't need to beg me to take her to the surface. She wasn't a prisoner. Hell, I'd give her my life if she asked. Still, my insecurity in losing her demanded something in return.

I stood, approached her back, and circled my arms around her tiny waist, careful not to let my erection brush against her. "I'll take you outside today, but I want a promise."

She turned to face me, her expression open, waiting.

"I want a kiss." What was I doing?

Do unto others what you want them to do to you. I doubted this was the Lord's intention. But with her body so close and her breath catching in her throat, nothing could've stopped me from cupping her beautiful face and leaning in. "It's just a kiss."

A kiss that would prove she felt this connection between us, that she needed me as much as I needed her, that she would fight her way back to me if something happened outside the safety of our bunker.

Her eyes closed, and her long lashes fringed the arches of her cheekbones. "Stop baiting me to do something you're not allowed to do."

I'd kissed her only once before, claiming we could show each other affection without making it about shagging. Because we were lonely. Because we no longer had family and friends to hold or care for. But I certainly hadn't kissed her the way I'd kissed my ma. Given the thoughts in my head and the ache in my cacks, I wanted to do a hell of a lot more than rub our mouths together.

Her eyes fluttered open. "I'll ruin you, Roark."

I'd never wanted to be ruined so thoroughly in my life, but I would wait for God to give me some direction, to help me find my way around, through, or inside this woman. "Put some faith in my control."

God forgive me, someone needed to.

When her lips separated and her little pink tongue darted out to wet the corner, I moved past wanting and dangerously skirted the edge of forcing. "Give me your mouth."

"Roark—"

"Now. Don't make me take it."

Her eyes dilated. "I don't know—"

"Stop talking and nod your head."

"Will it stop with just a kiss?" Her lips flattened into a line of hopeful hesitancy.

"I'll stop." God help me, I would have to. "Tell me *yes*, love."

Her hands fisted at her sides, her eyes darting away and returning to mine. "Yes." A whisper.

I slammed my mouth against hers, and she opened beneath my urgency. A heady submission, one that gripped me where I needed her most. I tried to keep it chaste and unassuming, but the moment our tongues touched, I angled her head and reached deep, licking and stretching my jaw until all I could feel was her breaths on my face and her supple flesh sliding beneath my lips.

She pressed her hands against my shoulders, and I braced for her to push away. Instead, her fingernails dug in, her mouth moving faster, mashing harder, needy and trembling. She was a burst of flavors, honeyed, dulcet, feminine, coating my tongue with the unmistakable taste of temptation.

I pulled her against me, savoring the hard bullets

of her nipples against my chest, soaking in her sensual affection until it scalded me from the inside out. I kept my hands on her lower back, fighting the instinct to slip beneath her shirt and grip the backs of her bare thighs. Feck me, she was so tiny, only a fraction of my size. Even if I could take this further, I'd break her in half trying.

She broke the kiss and stepped back, cheeks flushed and lips swollen. "That was…" She touched her mouth. "Priests aren't supposed to kiss like that."

"Priests aren't supposed to kill either." Yet I'd slaughtered my way through the U.K., decapitating men and monsters in self-defense. "The world has changed."

She glanced at the corridor, where the door to the outside world waited. "Ready to find out how much?"

TWO

I led Evie through the sewer pipes that connected the bunker to the surface. Then I put her on the back of my Harley Davidson and drove her through the decayed leftovers of South East England in search for clothes and survivors.

Not much had changed since the last time we ventured out. The buildings that once comprised the local parishes and villages were as inhabitable as the sarsen stones that dotted the rolling hilly moorland. Thatch roofs sank into the gaping husks of homes, foundations collapsed into gravel, and timber frames were scorched to ash. It was like the wreck of the Hesperus out here.

And the structures that had been sturdy enough to survive a year and a half of pillage and neglect were infected with man-sized pests. The kind of pests that had once been human.

When the plague first hit, news reporters called them aphids. The moniker stuck. Though, a cockroach reference would've been more fitting. Dirty, double-jointed, smelly-cunt cockroaches.

Sitting snug against my back on the bike, Evie

clutched a rifle against her side. A fur cloak enveloped most of her, but her arm trembled around my waist. The December chill could freeze off a brass monkey, and my trench coat and cassock did nothing to quell the speeding wind from biting into my bones.

I'd been motoring for over an hour, fairly tipping it along the barren roads, my gaze alert and gloved hands clenched on the handlebars. I hated the way the drone of the engine announced our approach. Nothing I could do about it as I zipped around fields and tors, yawing in and out of narrow alleyways between deteriorating buildings. As loud as the bike was, no one stepped out of their hidey-holes to greet us. At least, no one human.

Aphids skittered from overgrown farmland and decomposed dwellings. More insectile than human, the creatures always gave chase, the rumble of the bike and the scent of our blood calling them out of the shadows. With pincer-like hands swiping for flesh and mouthparts snapping for veins, their hard-shelled bodies blurred at inhuman speeds. Thankfully, they couldn't run as fast as the bike.

As much as I wanted to put them out of their misery, I didn't stop to engage them. Every time a snarl rent the air or a bulbous body emerged in my path, I opened the throttle with one thought on my mind. *Protect her.*

When we reached a hamlet of abandoned shops and homes, she tightened her arm around my waist. "Hold up." She pointed at a squatty house on the right. "Over there."

The front door was gone, but lacy curtains still hung in the windows, an indication that a woman had once lived there. God knew what occupied the space now.

I scanned the perimeter. Most of the buildings were gutted. Some burned. Others barely standing. But nothing moved. No signs of life on the road, in the surrounding fields, or stirring the shadows within the rubble.

The tires skidded as I slowed to a stop, the pavement moist and dewy from the persistent winter weather. I shut off the engine a few feet from the doorway, and for several minutes, I waited with my hand clenched on her thigh beside mine. I held her there, listening, observing, pacing my breaths with hers.

"It's safe." She pushed against my grip and swung off the bike. "I don't feel them."

Whatever it was about her biology that made her the only woman immune to the virus had also given her an uncanny ability to sense the infected.

"Sure, but you don't know if there are men nearby." I unsheathed the sword and matched her pace to the house, my neck craning side to side as I strained to see in every direction at once.

There wasn't a screed of gee left in the world. Lads were probably getting off with each other. If they saw her, they would tear each other apart to capture her, possess her, and hurt her.

"That's what I have this for." She tapped her fingers on the rifle and flashed me a grin.

How could her cockiness be so bloody sexy and

frustrating at the same time?

I caught her wrist and yanked her behind me, taking the lead through the doorway.

The stale scent of mold hung in the small space, and the wood floor groaned beneath my boots. A flurry of dust motes scattered in the bands of daylight streaming through the broken windows. A staircase led up, and a short hallway pointed to the kitchen.

"Up." She poked a finger against my spine. "The bedrooms."

My scalp itched as I climbed the first step. The rotting wood gave beneath my weight, spongy enough to fall apart.

I stabbed the sword in one of the planks. It didn't crumble, but it wanted to. Were new clothes worth risking a broken leg? We could abandon this home and try for another. Maybe the stairs wouldn't be as banjaxed elsewhere, but there were always worse things, such as sagging roofs, feral creatures, and the vomit-inducing aroma of decomposing bodies. The wet weather and disrepair of abandonment hadn't left a single building untouched. Every step in this godforsaken country was a fecking hazard.

I reached back and touched her waist. "Step where I step. We'll keep to the side."

She held the rifle against her shoulder, eyes glued to the doorway. I wasn't sure how she'd be able to aim and walk without tripping, but she managed it brilliantly, following my footfalls, moving when I moved. Until we reached the top.

With one foot on the landing, she doubled-over

and clutched her stomach, the gun dropping to her side as her face contorted in pain. "Roark. Shit."

She felt aphids. The sensation always gripped her in the gut, and given her sudden reaction, they were closing in fast.

I spun, reached for her arm, but she stumbled, seemingly disoriented. Her foot broke through a weak floorboard. The supports snapped, and the whole goddamned section dropped away, taking her with it.

My pulse thrashed as I dove for her, my hands slashing air, missing her by an inch. "Noooo!"

I caught my fall at the edge of the fissure and watched in horror as she plunged into the depths.

She landed one story below in a deafening explosion of dust and debris. As the clamor settled, a growl shuddered through the house. Followed by more growls, then the scrape of claws on wood. Silhouettes filled the doorway at the bottom of the stairs. Son of a pissing hell, I'd never reach her in time.

Lying on my chest, I stared down through the hole and frantically scanned her for injuries, for breath, for some indication of life. She sprawled on her back on a heap of rubble. Nothing pinned her down. I couldn't see blood. But she wasn't stirring.

"Evie? Evie, fuck, are you okay?" I couldn't breathe, couldn't move. My shout came out strained and choked. "Evie! Talk to me!"

She answered with a cough, but it didn't loosen the fist inside my chest. Not with the rifle tossed out of her reach. Too soon, the aphids would be on her, and all it took was one bite. A strike of their mouthparts, and she would become one of them.

"Evie!" I roared. "Get your arse up! Your gun's at your nine o'clock."

The stairs creaked with the approach of aphids. Five...six of the vicious buggers ascended quickly, their bulging egg-like eyes locked on me, and their mutated bodies quivering with hunger. Another dozen infiltrated the lower level, headed for Evie.

"Evie, they're coming!" I jumped up, careful of my footing, and double-fisted the sword.

The staircase splintered beneath taloned feet. A couple aphids staggered, screeching as their spiny legs broke through the rot. The others kept coming, strings of drivel clinging to their elongated mandibles.

Adrenaline heated my veins as I raised the sword, severed the head of the closest beast, and lurched forward to hew down the next. It turned its head. Our eyes locked, and its wide body sprung. I angled the sword and caught it in the chest, the sharp end punching clean through and out its back. But it wasn't dead. The head, the brain, whatever that disgusting lump was above the shoulders was the only way to kill it.

Yanking hard, my muscles protested as I freed the blade and cleaved through its neck. The head rolled off, and the body thudded at my feet.

The remaining four pulled themselves from the fractured stairs and flung toward me with rabid snarls and chomping jowls. But my focus was on the hole in the floor and the din of fast-moving creatures scurrying through the house.

"Evie!" I deflected an oncoming claw with my forearm, rammed my shoulder into the chest of another, and with a stab of the sword, I pierced the head of the fella on the stairs. "Evie, I'm coming!"

My jaw clamped to the point of pain, but when the sound of her grunting hit my ears, it felt as if I'd been punched in the gut. Were they biting her? Was she moving? My back was to the hole, the sword arcing around me. I swung with savage strikes, fueled with rage and urgency. Blood splattered my face, and bodies dropped. As the final head thumped down the stairs, several more aphids climbed their way up.

I whirled back toward the cavity in the floor. Twelve feet down, Evie sat against a tipped over refrigerator, flinging knives from the sheathes on her arms as three aphids blurred around her. They growled, and she hissed back, baring her teeth, chest heaving, and her daggers flying with remarkable accuracy.

My God, she was so gloriously ferocious it was arresting. But she wasn't standing, which meant she was injured.

I tossed the sword through the hole and leapt. My feet collided with the uneven pile of wood, and my legs gave out against the impact. I muscled through the jarring pain, scrambling for the sword. When my hand bumped the hilt, I jumped up and cut through the aphids surrounding her. The last one in the room dropped with a thump, and I leaned against the sword, fighting to fill my lungs.

She flashed me a grateful smile, but her mouth pulled tight at the corners.

I rushed toward her, my gaze sweeping over her denim-clad legs. "You're hurt."

"I'll live." Her hand grappled to collect the knife from the dead aphid beside her. "Behind you!"

I turned, let the sword fly in a wide sweep, decapitating another head. The hallway was our way to the front door, but it was crammed wall to wall with creatures. More were falling through the gap in the ceiling. I pivoted in a circle and spotted a back door.

Evie collected her knives and climbed to her feet, favoring her ankle and tripping over the carnage of timber and death. I snagged her rifle from the rubbish and grabbed her waist. She didn't fight me as I lifted her pint-sized body and tossed her over my shoulder.

"Hang on tight, love." I barreled through the back door and legged it to the corner of the house before the aphids flooded in from the front yard.

Squaring my shoulders, I sucked in a calming breath.

God, give me strength.

I clamped a hand over the backs of her thighs and sprinted through the horde, slicing and hacking a path to the bike. Gore clung to my skin. Bodies tumbled in my wake, and finally, I breached an opening and spun free of the fight.

Dropping Evie onto the bike, I kept the sword out and wheeling side to side, warding off jaws and talons within arm's reach. A low burn built in my shoulder from hefting the weight of the steel, and my lungs wheezed for air. There must've been twenty or thirty encircling us. How the hell would we make it out?

The sudden boom of her rifle ricocheted in my chest. She leaned over the bike seat, braced on her elbows, firing off brass and clearing a route for escape.

Aphids poured from the house and sprinted across the lawn. I straddled the bike and handed the sword back to her, which she sheathed in my scabbard as I fired the engine and sped off.

The swarm tailed us for miles, but eventually fell behind as the bike whined at top speeds.

The wind blinded me, whipping my hair in my eyes and chilling the sweat on my face. Evie gripped my chin-length dreadlocks, fisting the tangle at the back of my head. Her brow rested against my spine, and for the first time since we'd left the bunker, I let myself smile. I wouldn't have walked out of the house without her, even if it meant dying at her side. I didn't know what God thought of that, but I held Him responsible for sending her to me. If I didn't belong with her, I didn't belong anywhere.

We didn't stop until we reached the garage and didn't speak until we were safely in the underground sewer system. I cradled her against my chest, my boots slogging through the ankle-deep water. Icy drips fell from the ceiling, echoing from one end of the tunnel to the other. Murky shadows made it difficult to see, but I knew the way, having sloshed through these pipes countless times over the past year.

I'd checked her ankle before we left the garage. It was swollen, painful to the touch, but she didn't think it was broken.

She curled her fingers around my shoulder, and her gentle breaths on my neck chased away the tension in my muscles. "Guess I'll be borrowing your clothes."

I tipped my chin down, disappointed I couldn't see her gorgeous face in the dark. "What's mine is yours."

"Not *everything*."

No, not my body. At least, not in an intimate way.

I felt her shadowed gaze on my face, and I bet it looked a whole lot like a glare. "I want to give you that, too."

She blew out a breath and tightened her arms around me. "I know. God, Roark. *Knowing* you want to give me that makes the absence of it even more painful." She dropped her head on my chest. "I sound ungrateful. You've already given me so much. Thank you for saving me. Again."

My stomach clenched, every cell in my body aching to save her in a different way. To save her for myself. She had no idea how close I was to making her mine.

THREE

Like the gasps of a dying man, the weeks slipped by, each one counted, cherished, and needful. Holed up in the bunker, we tried to keep ourselves busy. I taught Evie how to swing a sword, and she taught me Jiu-Jitsu. The techniques were useful for self-defense, but ground wrestling with her was a blessed misery. With her toned body grinding against mine, flexing and panting in a tangle of limbs, how could I not think about fucking her all the damned time?

We'd attempted another excursion to the surface and managed to collect a few books from a nearby library. She'd wanted research on the biology of aphids. But the errand had ended as sorry and stressful as the last, and I'd been forced to kill two human men who tried to hurt her. I'd be happy if we never left the bunker again.

I prepared all her meals, looked forward to it, to hearing the soft moans of pleasure that escaped her lips as she chewed. It made me want things, but I limited myself to touching, something I did more than I should have. We'd become so comfortable with one another, sharing every second together, modesty fell away. In its place emerged an intimacy I'd never experienced with another person.

I'd always been friendly with the ladies. A little innocent affection went a long way in a celibate life. But there was nothing saintly about my relationship with Evie. Every brush of my fingers, lingering look, and word I spoke vibrated with yearning. The kind of intense, demanding need I'd never allowed myself to entertain. I fought it. Bloody *hell*, I fought it. Tried to smother it with exercise, prayer, and guilt. But my feelings overpowered my intentions.

Like now.

I lay in bed, awake again, both of us nude from the waist up, as my gaze followed the slope of her back from inches away. The natural perfume of her skin infiltrated my inhales, and the seductive lines of her body burned into my eyes. She was all I saw, smelled, and thought about. Every moment with her was heaven.

And hell.

Her breaths whispered through the room, soft, steady. I loved to caress her while she slept. It didn't ease the guilt, but it spared me the accusations I so often found in her eyes.

Dragging my lips across her shoulder, I tried to keep my whiskers from scratching her satiny flesh. She slept nude most nights since she didn't own many clothes. The body contact kept us warm beneath the blankets, and I tried to be respectful and not stare at the parts of her I couldn't touch. At least, not while she was looking.

I trailed fingers over the bumps of her spine, and my mouth found her nape. I couldn't pull away. Her scent, heat, vulnerability, everything about her was addictive. With my arm around her waist and my knee tucked between her thighs, I gentled my kisses across her neck, careful not to wake her.

Her body seemed to melt against me, surrendering even in sleep. What would it feel like to grow hard beneath the stroke of her hands? To slide my fingers between her legs? To thrust inside her mouth? I wouldn't last long. Just thinking about it tightened my stomach and engorged my cock with pulsing heat.

"Roark?"

I jerked my lips from her neck. Feck me arseways, how long had the little harpy been awake? What must she think of me, kissing and fondling her body without asking? My face burned with shame, and the rest of me screamed with aching frustration.

After a few heavy heartbeats, I shifted, rolling her to face me. I tried to unclench my jaw and blink away the desire I knew she could see in my eyes. The same look she gave me.

We stared at one another, nose to nose, neither of us moving to break apart or close the distance. When she licked her lips, the muscles in my stomach clenched, rippled lower, and settled into a throb along my swollen dick. The unrequited ache inside me was unbearable, quickening by the second, but I'd made a promise to God. Which meant there was no relief in sight.

Except she hadn't taken a vow, and as she stared up at me, eyes dark with hunger, I knew this wouldn't end gently.

She drew a deep breath, the words delivered on her exhale. "Please. Fuck me."

God, I don't ask you to make this easier, but please give me the power to do the right thing. She's important. I know this. But I can't ignore the feeling that she's more important than my vow. Please give me a sign of acknowledgment.

Weeks of pent-up need shook through my body. Just a kiss. A touch. God would understand.

I buried a hand in her soft hair, knotting a shock of it at her nape. My other hand swept around her hip as I pressed my mouth hard against hers. When my tongue slipped past her lips, a trail of fire tore through me. She fell into my kiss, clinging to me as tightly as I clung to her. Instinct propelled me to climb on top of her, trapping her breathy body beneath me as I ate at her mouth, seeking her tongue, and nudging the hard length of my arousal between her legs.

My hunger for her was overwhelming, swelling inside me, and demanding release. I'd been attracted to plenty of women over the years, but none of them had affected me like this. None of them made me feel so fecking out of control, thrashing against the fetters of my vow. Maybe that was the sign I'd been waiting for. Maybe I felt this way because this was God's purpose? Maybe He'd sent her to me so I could love her in all ways?

No, I was delusional, making excuses so I

wouldn't feel guilty about giving into this…this sinful lust.

I released her mouth and leaned back, searching her eyes.

"I want you." My fingers molded to the contour of her waist and wandered over the edge of her bare breast. "You don't know how much I want…but I—"

"No," she whispered between clenched teeth. "We both want this. Please."

I squeezed my eyes shut and curled my hand into a fist on her chest. I needed to put space between us. Right now.

My entire body constricted as I shifted away.

"No." She rolled after me, restrained by twisted bedding.

I scooted to the end of the bed, hunched over, the ache in my groin robbing my ability to think. My hands shook violently, fighting the urge to stroke her, finger her, make her scream with desire. "God forgive me."

"God forgive you?" She growled at my back. "Bullshit. What about me forgiving you?"

My stomach dropped. I didn't deserve her forgiveness.

"Fuck this." She untangled her legs from the blankets and bolted to the bathroom, gloriously naked, the perfect shape of her arse flexing with her strides.

"Evie!" I grabbed a shirt for her from the floor and a pair of pants for me and ran after her.

She slammed the door and sent something crashing to the floor behind me.

My chest collapsed. I'd started this, woke her with my selfish need to explore her body with no intention of taking care of *her* needs. I wouldn't blame her if she cut me while I slept.

The dismay that had drawn her expression was enough to douse my arousal. I pulled the trousers on over my briefs, sat on the cold concrete outside of the bathroom, and leaned against the frame. The rustling of her movements muffled through the door, the sounds floating from the floor. I flattened a hand against the wood, imagining her in the same position on the other side.

As worked up as she'd been, I wondered if she was touching herself. She masturbated daily, right there on the floor behind this door. I'd heard her moans, caught her flushed cheeks when she emerged, and sometimes I asked her about it. She always gave it to me straight. Her unashamed honesty was one of the countless things I loved about her.

Eventually she would come out, calm and forgiving. At least self-pleasure would take the edge off her pain. My vow didn't allow me that.

God, I'm afraid. I don't want to fail you. Or her. Please help me understand my role in her life. I want to guard her not harm her. Please show me how to love her without disappointing you.

The longer we remained confined to the bunker, the more these feelings between us would strain. I swore to protect her, asking only for her faith in my discipline. But I was hurting her in the process.

A shadow flickered under the bathroom door.

The knob wobbled, and the door swung open.

She sat on the other side, legs straight out and crossed at the ankles, her back to the wall.

I resisted the impulse to stare at her nudity and held out the shirt I'd grabbed for her. "I'm sorry. You deserve more."

"Don't be sorry. I didn't mean what I said." Her accent was sweet, but bitterness sharpened the syllables.

I watched as she pulled the shirt on, her jaw stiff and resolute. If I could only be as strong as she was.

She scooted toward me and leaned against the opposite side of the doorway, her gaze thoughtful.

When I draped an arm over my bent knee, she hooked her pinky around my thumb. "What do you pray for?"

I stared at our hands, relishing the connection. "Forgiveness, guidance, strength...you."

"But you can't have me." Her chest hitched. "We should sleep separately."

"No." I interlaced our fingers. "Sleeping with my arms around you is my favorite part of every day. I won't have it another way."

I trusted God to guide me in my weakest moments, but the thing was, with Evie I wasn't weak. She strengthened my heart, filled me with fight, and reminded me I was alive. I just needed to be patient. God would show me the way.

Two weeks later, He did.

FOUR

I woke with a strange feeling creeping over my skin. A quick glance around the bunker confirmed we were alone. Safe. Evie lay beside me, eyes closed in sleep. But I couldn't shake this odd sensation that something was happening. Something chilly and mysterious, like a ghostly presence in the air. I bolted up and slid off the mattress, groggy and confused.

On the bed, blankets cocooned her, but that wasn't all. A tiny bug perched on her arm. Not just any bug. *A ladybird.*

I'd lived here over a year and had never had a pest problem. In fact, I hadn't seen a ladybird since before the plague.

Tugging on a pair of jeans, I paced around the bed and scanned the ceiling and dark corners of the room for an entrance point, an infested hole where more might've been congregating. But the bunker was bug-free. Except the bed, and the little red body that hovered around Evie.

I had very specifically asked for a sign from God, an acknowledgment that she was more sacred than my vow.

HEART OF EVE

The ladybird was named after the Blessed Lady, the Virgin Mary. It was believed that the red wings represented her cloak and the black spots her sorrows. Not only that, every gardener in the U.K. used these beetles to combat the sap-sucking, plant-destroying insects otherwise known as aphids.

The sign from God couldn't have been clearer.

I knelt on the mattress beside her, shaking her shoulders. "Evie. Evie."

Her lashes fluttered up. "Mm?"

"Did you read any of your entomology texts? Or any of the books on aphids?"

She closed her eyes and waved me away. "Tomorrow."

"I read them." I shook her again. "Evie? Do you know what the aphid's biggest predator is?"

"My 5.56 round between the eyes."

She was savagely sexy with the gun, but that wasn't how I imagined her now. I was getting ahead of myself, but I held onto this sign from God with both fists as I pictured her beneath me, her body flexing, legs spread, and her soft flesh wrapped around my cock.

I hooked my hands under her armpits and slid her to a sitting position. Curling a knuckle under her chin, I lifted her eyes to mine. Even in the dim candlelight, her golden gaze stole my breath. "Aphids. The wee insects. Do you know their predator, love?"

She yawned, barely opening her eyes.

I put my face in hers and gripped her neck. "Ladybirds. The bloody aphids' predators are ladybirds."

The air seemed to have vacated the room. I tried to rein in my excitement, but my breaths grew shorter, faster. Sitting back on my ankles, I waited for her to notice the red and black body fluttering around her.

Her gaze landed on it, tracking it for a sleepy moment. Then she jumped out of the bed and swatted her hand. "Oh God, where did it come from?"

"Exactly." I ran a hand over my mouth, my heart pumping with wonderment and veneration. "You are hallowed."

Her eyes widened. "You can't be serious."

I stood still, hands to my sides, watching the unnatural way the beetle gravitated toward her, undeterred by her waving hand. "This is big. Bigger than us."

Before humans had mutated into insectile creatures, I wouldn't have given the presence of a ladybird a single thought. But this wasn't just a bug. It was the message I pleaded for. I could love her how I wanted. I could offer her what she needed. God had given me His blessing.

My pulse quickened as I visually took her in, letting myself really absorb her feminine form without shame. Her breasts sat high and round beneath the shirt, her legs strong and slender as she shifted from foot to foot. She always carried herself with confidence, her shoulders back and fortified with courage, no matter what she faced. She was rare, precious, gorgeous in every sense of the word, and tonight I would know every flawless part of her.

Anxiousness curled in my gut. What if I fumbled

my way through it and turned her off? What if I was too rough? What if she said *no*?

Didn't matter. I wanted her heart and intended to earn it.

FIVE

I followed Evie to the couch, listening to her argue the ridiculousness of my logic. She thought I was teasing her. Flirting around an idea that could never come to fruition. Of course, she did. She didn't believe in God, didn't subscribe to vows or miracles. Why would she think anything had changed? I would have to prove to her I wouldn't be stopping tonight.

But I let her say what she had to say. I could listen to her accent all night, the lazy drawl of her words, the way she licked her lips during pauses, it was seductive and hypnotizing.

From her curled up position on the couch, she watched me the way I watched her, her eyes wandering over my bare chest, lingering on the mold of my jeans. When they came back to rest on my face, they were molten gold, burning with want.

I crawled over her and kicked her knees out with my legs. Then I settled my hips between her thighs, letting her fully feel the iron strength of my desire.

"I surrender." I breathed against her mouth. "If I were honest, I surrendered the day I met you."

"Stop. Shit." She pushed me away and jumped

from the couch. "You told me to trust your discipline. Despite all your teasing, I did trust you. And now you're ready to forgo it? Just like that?"

I wasn't sure what my expression held. Maybe my determination was parading all over my face, because her eyes softened and her hands fell to her sides. The air between us shifted, sizzled, charged.

I rose from the couch and stepped toe-to-toe with her, a nervous smile twitching my lips.

Her hand went to the low waistline of her sweatpants. To hold them in place? Or to take them off? "What are you—?"

I showed her with a kiss. Irish whiskey flavored our tongues as I teased her lips apart. My already rapid pulse surged through my veins, my cock hard and painfully trapped in my jeans. Her fingers gripped my biceps as I thrust deeper into her mouth, losing myself to the wet heat of her lips.

With a groan, I pulled away. "Of all the carnal temptations over the years, I've never wavered. Do you know why it's different with you?"

She gave me an excruciatingly beautiful smile. "Holing up with the world's last lass for endless weeks might have something to do with it."

Those had been my words, and they sounded strangely adorable and sexy in her American accent.

"Nah, love. Let me show you."

I lifted her hand, balancing my fingertips against hers, then slid them over her palm, up her forearm to the inside of her elbow. Goosebumps trailed the electric touch. I did it again, only this time I guided her fingers over my palm, my arm, her caress mimicking mine.

Static skated my skin, lifting the hairs on my arms. It made my whole body tremble. "Do you feel that?"

She swallowed, nodded, and swallowed again.

I nodded too, padding a finger across her lips. She let me raise her hand and mirror the movement on me. Her finger was so soft against my lips, so inviting. I was more aware of my body than I'd been in my life. I didn't just feel her on my skin. I felt her inside me.

I pressed my palm over her heart, and she followed suit. Her beat under my hand thumped in chorus with mine. This was where I belonged.

Hooking a finger in her waistband, I yanked her body flush with mine. When she gasped, I used her surprise to capture her mouth.

Sweet Jesus, she felt good, her tongue rubbing against mine, her hips rocking and grinding. I wanted her. Bloody hell, I'd never needed someone so badly. My cock ached to be freed, throbbing like a second heartbeat, but it wasn't just that. I wanted to meld with her, to burrow under her skin the way she'd sneaked under mine. She was the center of my existence. This wasn't just surrender. It was devotion. Willingly, gratefully, I gave myself to her, and she gave right back.

I wanted to hear her gasp, so I gripped her firm butt and pulled her against me in a needy grind over my rigid shaft.

She didn't just gasp, she breathed hot and husky into my mouth. "Don't stop."

A wave of relief surged through me. She'd moved past questioning the status of my vow and had put her desire in my hands. It only made me want her more.

Lips locked in urgency, we shuffled toward the bed and tumbled onto the mattress, laughing into our kiss, neither of us willing to separate our mouths.

With shaking fingers, I tore at the elastic of her pants. Cotton stretched as I shoved it down her legs. I couldn't be gentle. I was thirty-two pent-up years past gentle. I couldn't focus on anything but spreading her thighs and rutting between them, to find refuge in a place I'd never been. But I knew I would love it there. I knew I'd never want to leave.

The bunker filled with the rip and rustle of shed clothes as we stripped each other with desperate, jerking movements. Finally naked, our hands explored. Hers on my chest, tracing the lines of my muscles to my back and dipping into the cleft of my arse. My hands closed around her breasts, the heavy flesh overfilling my palms. Perfectly shaped, with hard pink nipples pointing upward, begging for my tongue. Greedily, I latched on, sucking and nipping while rubbing my cock against her inner thigh.

She moaned, rocking with me, her back bowing off the mattress and her fingers tangling in my dreadlocks. I reached down between her legs, desperate to feel the part of her I'd fantasized about for so long. My fingers found her wet heat, slipping through the delicate folds, and my hunger detonated with unrestrained urgency.

I attacked her mouth, licking and biting, wanting more, more, until…Ahhh God, my finger sank inside her, drenched and gripped by tight muscles. I thrust my hand, miming sex, making sure she knew my intent.

I raised my body, panting, as I watched my fingers move between her legs. In and out. Round and round.

"So soft. Slick." My eyes flicked to hers, my voice thick with need. "Sacred."

Just touching her like this escalated my hunger. I grunted against her mouth, humped and rubbed against her thigh, as I fucked her with my hand. I needed in her, and I needed it now.

Something shifted in her eyes. Hesitancy? Uncertainty? Was she thinking about my vow? I wasn't, but it would serve me right if she stopped this now after all the sexual frustration I'd put her through.

She grabbed my face, cold hands on my heated cheeks. "This can't come between us. Understand?"

I twisted my lips in a lopsided grin and lined up my hips, replacing my fingers with my aching cock. Christ, I was shaking from head to toe, straining against the impulse to thrust. But I paced myself, drawing out every movement, committing each stimulation to memory. I slipped my wet fingers into her mouth and watched, mesmerized, as she tasted her arousal.

When her suckling lips became intolerable, I shoved my hand in her hair, knotting and pulling, and held on tightly.

"This…" I pressed the head of my cock against her opening and tried to remember to breathe. "This *will* come between us."

Then I thrust.

Every thought, every sensation, every pulse point in my body narrowed on where we were joined. It was unlike anything I'd ever imagined. Indescribable. Overwhelming. Fucking hell, I wanted to come instantly.

The moment I started moving, I couldn't stop. The pressure inside me heated and swelled, threatening to explode.

My head dropped, cheek stroking cheek, the tendons in my neck straining from the onslaught of pleasure. "Uhh...unngh."

Thrust after thrust, I drove my hips like an animal. My muscles felt supercharged, surging with life and heated with exertion. I was so fucking hard I felt like I was stabbing her with a sword. But the look on her face was one of pure bliss. Bright eyes. Flushed cheeks. Parted lips. I put that look there, and fuck did that turn me on.

Our tongues collided, tangled, and I was gone. Lost in the thrumming of heartbeats, panting breaths, and rolling hips. So fecking gone, my thighs shook with the need to spend.

"Oh, love. Oh, Evie. This is—" A shudder went through me. I was going to come. I was right there, holding on by a thread, but I didn't want this to end. Buried inside her, I leaned up, wrestling with my breaths. "I can't..."

"No, you don't. Not now." She hooked her legs around my back and dug her heels into the backs of my thighs.

She thought I was going to pull away?

I released a shaky laugh and pinned her writhing hips to the mattress, stilling her movements. "Just need a minute, love."

A relieved smile bowed her lips.

I held still, firmly seated inside her, as we stared at one another, ragged breaths mingling, the intimate connection magnifying the anticipation. It took me a moment to get a grip on my control. I wouldn't last much longer, but I hoped to last long enough to make her come. I sat up and hauled her to me, chest to chest. With my arms coiled around her back and my mouth on hers, I began to move.

She rocked in my lap, calves sawing against my back. We found a rhythm, and the wicked pleasure of her clenching muscles hurdled me toward the precipice. My body tensed, prepared to unfurl. Our tongues disentangled.

"Come with me," I mouthed.

She tightened her arms around my neck. She was there, clamping around my cock and nodding her head.

I pushed forward, pressed her back against the mattress, and unleashed the full force of my need, driving my hips, groaning, trembling, ready to fall off the ledge. "Now."

Her pupils reacted, and her head tilted back as her cry rent the air. Holy Mother of God, I could feel her spasming around my thrusts. It was my undoing.

My orgasm burst from me, tearing a strangled groan from my throat, my hips locked up, my body rigid beneath the unimaginable ecstasy. For an eternal heartbeat, I wondered if I'd died. What a way to go.

I lay there, reluctant to leave the warm clutch of her body, floating in a hinterland between dreams and reality. I'd given her my virginity, my vow, my heart. I didn't take that lightly but neither did she. At some point in the past couple months, she'd fallen in love with *me*, a man, a priest, and she would've continued to love me with or without my cock inside her.

As the pulse in her chest beat against mine, I knew I hadn't lost my vow. I gained a new one.

She was my vow.

Mine to protect.

She was my strength.

Mine to love.

She was my heart.

Mine to fight for.

This is just a taste of the world and characters in the Trilogy of Eve.

If you would like to read more about Evie and her guardians, her story begins with:
DEAD OF EVE, Book 1.

Book 1 is a woman's survival story and takes its time building the romance.
Book 2 is the most erotic book I've written to date.
The world-building, the cast of characters, the meaningful and inconsolable love between Evie and three men, and the terrifying, thought-provoking, emotional journey... This series is by far my favorite of all my books.

TRILOGY OF EVE
Dead of Eve #1
Blood of Eve #2
Dawn of Eve #3

OTHER BOOKS BY PAM GODWIN

LOVE TRIANGLE ROMANCE
TANGLED LIES TRILOGY
One is a Promise
Two is a Lie
Three is a War

DARK ROMANCE
DELIVER SERIES
Deliver #1
Vanquish #2
Disclaim #3
Devastate #4
Take #5
Manipulate #6
Unshackle #7
Dominate #8
Complicate #9

DARK COWBOY ROMANCE
TRAILS OF SIN
Knotted #1
Buckled #2
Booted #3

STUDENT–TEACHER / PRIEST
Lessons In Sin

STUDENT–TEACHER ROMANCE
Dark Notes

ROCK-STAR DARK ROMANCE
Beneath the Burn

ROMANTIC SUSPENSE
Dirty Ties

EROTIC ROMANCE
Incentive

DARK HISTORICAL PIRATE ROMANCE
King of Libertines
Sea of Ruin

ABOUT PAM GODWIN

New York Times and USA Today Bestselling author, Pam Godwin, lives in the Midwest with her husband, their two children, and a foulmouthed parrot. When she ran away, she traveled fourteen countries across five continents, attended three universities, and married the vocalist of her favorite rock band.

Java, tobacco, and dark romance novels are her favorite indulgences, and might be considered more unhealthy than her aversion to sleeping, eating meat, and dolls with blinking eyes.

EMAIL: pamgodwinauthor@gmail.com

Made in the USA
Middletown, DE
11 July 2024

57187273R00031